Sia Air Ochd

Six by Eight

Foreword

The ninth book in the series of poetic wanderings through the stones of time and Into the Outlander Series. Written as a homage to the novels of Diana Gabaldon and the content of the Starz TV series.

The author has interpreted the series in poems and rhyme, with a ribald sense of humour and a deep respect of the original material. These poems have featured on several social media groups and have become a coffee time institution.

This book has now wandered into the eight episodes which comprise series six. Hence the title.

Take a view of the Christie family in rhyme and experience life on Frasers Ridge in poetry. The love life of Lizzie Wemyss and the narrow-minded gossip of the fisher folk.

They will take all that they have been encouraged to build in their community and destroy It with their superstitions and their Ignorance.

This book will hold the essence of series 6 In your heart and mind until series 7.

Read on and enjoy.

The author is a volunteer with Riding for the Disabled and donates all revenue to this worthy cause.

COVER IMAGE EDIT CREDITED TO Hanca Forch

A BIT ABOUT RDA: Our horses benefit the lives of over 25,000 disabled children and adults. With fun activities like riding and carriage driving, we provide therapy, fitness, skills development, and opportunities for achievement – all supported by 18,000 amazing volunteers and qualified coaches at nearly 500 RDA centres all over the UK.

RDA is an inclusive and diverse organisation. We welcome clients with physical and learning disabilities and autism, and there are no age restrictions.

Through our network of member groups, RDA is at work in every corner of the UK, in our cities and remote rural areas, bringing the therapy, achievement and fun of horses to as many people as we can.

We are a charity, and we can only carry out our life-changing activities thanks to the generosity of our donors, the dedication of our volunteers and the good nature of our fantastic horses.

Contents

Flash Back to Ardsmuir
Start of Season 6

Jenny knew me taken,
That had been the plan,
I could na stand tae live my life,
Devoid of any man.

They would take the English coin,
The price upon my head,
I would go to prison
Or I'd end up dead.

Fettered tight and in a cart,
No escape for me,
They can'nae lose Red Jamie,
They brought me here by sea.

The lurching hold, below the deck,
The rolling of the swell
I puked until I thought I'd die
I looked as green as hell.

I crawled in chains under a bench,
Away from all around,
I wished a hole would open up,
And take me neath the ground.

The cell floor moved, alive with rats,
The stone was damp and cold,
Shivers rattled all my bones,
Here I would grow old.

A place so bleak to break a man,
Without having to endure,
Christie's pious preaching,
Welcome to Ardsmuir

The Ballad of James McCready (s6 e1)

Groping hands-on filthy floor,
Searching in the dark,
Eyes grown weak through lack of light,
Young – yet to make his mark.

A lock of hair, a precious thing
A tie with loved ones lost,
A locket one last token thing
Reminds him of the cost.

A stuttering apology,
Sir, I'm going blind,
Memory of his young wife's face,
He cannot bring to mind.

Christie bids me think of God,
Soldier for his cause,
Have we lost all for nothing then?
Must we accept these laws.

I hear men say your wife is 'gone'
But you remember well,
How do you keep her memory?
Mine is a broken spell,

Close your eyes, you'll see her,
Her image will come in
We have loved like others can't,
That cannot be a sin.

Comfort given in the dark,
To men with whom he bled,
And in the bitter feuding,
James McCready dead,

Here's a bit o'tartan
To take ye to yer grave,
Someone must be punished
For Auld Charlie's act sae brave.

Tis mine – the voice commanded,
Once more he shed his sark,
Christie saw the silvered scars,
Which marked his back like bark!

Silently he took the lash,
Instead of that poor fool,
And quietly the Ardsmuir men
Came back under his rule.

Tom Christie cannot see it,
He'd have auld Charlie flogged,
This is not justice Fraser.
The answer – Is it not!

The Pope is nae in Ardsmuir
In Prison with my men
There is a supreme being
In my beliefs ye ken.

Become a lodge of Masons
Quarry saw the point,
Leaving Thomas Christie
A nose well out of joint.

Stones of Ardsmuir (s6 e1)

Broken, beaten, worn with work
Preached at every day,
Enough tae drive a sane man mad,
Not follow Gods good way.

Inflated like a big wee toad,
Spouting for his Lord,
The more he shouts the less they heed
Any of his words.

A man may work his self tae death,
With peat and heavy rocks,
But constant penance on his ears,
Is one too many shocks.

What point to fight between ourselves?
We need a common ground,
This wee proud man will spread dissent
No peace will e'er be found.

And Quarry is a yes man,
He'd like a quiet life,
Get this posting over with,
Avoid all form of strife!

A handshake with a subtlety,
A level and a square,
The Pope is not in Ardsmuir,
As if he'd think I care.

A prison lodge of masons,
Forbids the men to fight,
No politics, no talk of gods,
And we'll have peace tonight.

Deflated, with his nose put out,
His pride would fester long,
Those cold stone walls won't chill his ire,
His preaching will go on.

To all the men of Ardsmuir
Come settle on the Ridge
A home so far from Scotland,
Your common bond a bridge

Here he came, with Fisher folk
To settle on my land
Still preaching loud to burn yer ears,
A Bible in his hand.

Listen hard and listen well,
There's welcome here for sure,
Tom Christie ye will keep the peace,
For here my word is law.

A Broken Family (s6 e1)

Once confined in Ardsmuir,
Indentured with the rest,
The stores man for the Jacobites,
He thought himself the best,

Set himself as leader,
The only man of letters,
Severe in his religion,
A man not kept in fetters.

A man without a presence,
A man without command,
He had never raised a sword,
To fight at Charlie's hand.

They'd found Red Jamie Fraser,
They brought him in by night,
Seasick from the journey,
And chained, lest he fight.

Revered by all, a hero
A leader to his core
An Officer, a papist
A warrior for sure.

And so began a certain rift
Of petty jealousy,
Tom Christie's nose put out of joint
For all the men to see.

Mac Duh – son of the Black one
They'd follow him til death,
Inspiring of loyalty,
With every captive breath.

Seeking refuge on the ridge,
Christie swallowed pride,
Made a home amongst them
His family at his side.

His family, who were they,
Who knew he had a wife,
And children left abandoned,
Neglected, scarred for life.

A son who raised his sister,
Without a moral stitch
They who watched their mother swing,
Convicted as a Witch

The Plan (s6 e1)

Brother you were always there
Yet I sense you do me wrong
It is not right the things you do,
Yet I play along.

Father will not suffer this
It was not in the plan,
I fear I am got with child,
And yes – you are the man.

Fraser, he has money
Lure him to your side,
He is a man, he won't resist,
Soon you could be his bride.

Betray his wife, she is a witch,
We can see her dead,
Once she's gone, he'll claim his child
That's more jam for our bread.

So, I watched and waited,
Collected what I'd need,
The way he took his woman
His passion in the deed.

When you've lived a life of lies
The truth is hard to see,
No way in god's universe
Would he fall in love with me

I knew the script, I learned it well,
I backed it up with fact,
A mire so deep in evil
I never can retract.

Allan plays the outrage,
I play the wounded soul
Comfort his darkest hours
My heart as black as coal.

Stiff with white hot anger,
Quiet pent-up rage,
This man, who offered kindness
Stepped onto the stage

He called my lies, he called me whore
I nearly lost my nerve,
He promised I would tell the truth,
Or get what I'd deserve.

Understanding Men (s6 e1)

Both had been imprisoned,
Both honourable men,
Neither one will give an inch.
Like rams fenced in a pen,

Butting heads, a contest,
Which one is the stronger,
I'd bet Mr Fraser,
Will last out the longer,

I'd sewn up Tom Christie's hand,
With no pain relief,
With Jamie there he would not flinch
He'd groan through gritted teeth,

They play a game of cat and mouse,
Verbal barbs, and taunts,
One mentions honour in his scars,
One Bible knowledge flaunts.

Each testing the other,
They fight with verbal swords,
Who will Lose their cool to temper?
In this game of words,

Christie has the last word
Going through the door,
But Jamie's laughing – eyebrow raised,
He's seen it all before.

Opposite in many ways,
But really just the same,
Men like Christie needed,
If we are to win the game.

I don't think I can understand,
Why they never stop
The constant competition,
The need to be on top.

Sassenach don't fool yourself,
You ken us all too well,
You'd like to think you din'nae,
For it is the road to hell.

Tom Christie is a fighter,
When his nose is out of joint,
He'll fight hard to keep his place,
And that is just the point.

The Mask of Sleep (s6 e1)

Sweet sleep
A few drops on the mask
Perhaps a few drops more
Erase the pictures from the past,
The pain you can't ignore

Breathe deep
To lie oblivious
If only for a while
Blank out the racing of your mind
Blot out all that's vile

Sweet dreams
Ride on waves of hope
Hide away from life
Refuge here from darkness
Refuge here from strife

Inhale
Descend into the depths
Picture all you love
Shut out the hurt, shut out the pain,
Let that go on above.

One drop more
Will take you there
One sweet drop on the mask
One drop to oblivion
If that is what you ask

He calls you
Do not spoil the rush,
Don't let him see your cure
secrecy imperative
If these dreams are to endure

He wakes you
From my cloying fumes
He breaks sweet smelling dreams
Pulls you to reality
Did he not hear your screams?

Secrets
You make room for me,
For me to him you lie
Convince him you are in control
I will not let you die

Don't Listen
You are deaf to him
I've stolen all your pain
Locked it in my walls of glass
And you will seek me again

Next time
I will call you
When nightmares ring your bell
Sweet sleep in a bottle
I am the road to hell

The Devils Genes – (s6 e1)

Lucifer – light bearer
Mistress, what's it for?
Phosphorus glows in oxygen,
The devils light for sure,

A mind confused by preaching,
Mixed with superstition,
Earnest eyes seek answers,
What really is her mission?

Instructed how to fear her god,
Not taught more than she needs
Religion, history, and prayer
Just who planted this seed.

He does not teach her science,
Her curious mind might light,
What's in her bone and in her blood
Just may win that fight.

She has no fear of seeing death,
She seeks control of life,
I could teach her healing,
But her father would cause strife.

He is a man of learning,
Why does he hold her back?
What does he fear is in this child?
That makes her outlook black.

Her dabbling in science,
Helping with my healing,
Her interest in macabre things,
He sees the devils dealing.

Time will tell the story,
Tom will spill the beans,
His wife, her mother was a witch
She has the devils' genes!

One Hand – (s6 e1)

Milord has kept the oath he made,
To him I am a son,
Married to his daughter,
Hands – I have but one!

I am not a farmer,
I cannot work the land,
There is nothing on The Ridge,
For a Frenchman with one hand.

My wife is always pregnant,
But I cannot provide,
Scornful when she looks at me,
It makes me die inside.

Tis she that tends the children,
And she that tends the beasts,
The house, the home, she cooks and cleans
And I contribute least.

Her kinfolk think me lazy,
Or look at me with pity
A Frenchman born and Paris bred
I'm better in the city.

My refuge is the Whisky still,
A place where I can hide,
Taste the product as it's made,
Liquor now my bride.

A black cloud lives over my head,
It permeates my soul,
Nothing will bring lightness back,
Oblivion my goal.

When all around are toiling,
I'm drunk - can barely stand,
I am ashamed, I am no use,
I only have one hand.

Things I know are said in jest,
Are arrows to my heart,
Dark despair has landed,
Never to depart.

Fergus, do not work so hard,
Sampling the wares.
Marsali needs you home with her,
She's worn away with cares.

Fergus, watch the weans,
Fergus milk the goat,
This Is not work for a man
Man's work should be of note!

Milord is losing patience,
For he sees a lot,
And now he sees his son of heart,
Become a drunken sot

Fisher Folk – (s6 e1)

My Da was of the fisher folk
We din'nae farm the land,
Fishermen not hunters
No rifle in our hand.

We travelled to the Colonies,
To start our lives anew,
On the way my Da died,
What are we to do?

Now there's only me and Ma
And my little brother
I'm scared I want my old home,
I do not want another.

This new place is in the trees,
So far from the sea,
How will we fare, what will we do?
My brother, Ma, and me

Tom Christie is a scary man
He'd have us build for God,
We have no roof above our heads,
He does nae think that odd.

Mr Frasers word is law
He welcomes us to stay,
But we must build cabins
Before a place to pray

They give us food, they find us clothes
For those that have the least
Invite us to their big fine house
There is to be a feast.

I want to run away and hide,
I sit upon the stairs,
A big man with a big black beard,
The friendliest of stares

Tells me I'm a man now
I must look out for Ma
And he'll help us build a cabin
Cos, I din nae have a Da.

He bid me eat and drink my fill
Make ourselves at home
To see my Ma her face lit up
A cabin of her own.

And there are many of children
Lots of us to play
Maybe I could like this place,
Yes – me and Ma will stay!

Written for Caleb Reynolds who plays Aiden
MacCallum in Season six

Come Back Sassenach (s6 e2)

Sassenach, I worry,
It is nae sitting well,
The sleep ye seek, unnatural,
Yet ye fall under its spell,

I ken yer mind is troubled,
Tell me what is wrong
A trouble shared; a trouble halved
With two we're twice as strong.

I feel ye leave my side at night
Ye creep around the house,
Ye think ye do it quiet,
But yer too large for a mouse.

Talk to me, tell me your pain,
Let us talk it through,
Don't lock away your demons,
For then they stay with you.

When I awake, and you are gone,
ye've sneaked off to that place
Yer chemical oblivion
With that mask o'er yer face.

The space I feel beside me,
Cold under the covers,
Do not let your shadows,
Force us apart as lovers.

Answer me please Sassenach
I beg ye tell me why,
I fear for our future,
I fear that you may die.

Time will dim the demons,
Forgiveness numbs the pain,
I would kill them all fer you,
To have ye back again.

I will not let ye do this,
Once you saved my soul,
Shall I stop ye making ether,
If that will keep ye whole.

I can nae lie alone at night,
Where once ye laid yer head,
Reaching out for comfort,
In a cold and empty bed.

Matches (s6 e2)

Lit up with excitement,
A tiger poised to pounce
Brianna's eyes are fiery proud,
She's something to announce.

Jumping to conclusions,
Suspense will drive them wild,
Please calm down, the lot of you!
I am not 'with child'

Lucifer light bearer
Phosphorus in the dark
Exposed to air it will ignite
Without even a spark

Fire at your fingertips
Flames upon a stick,
Easier than striking flint
When you light a wick.

Tumbleweed went round the room
Why would that excite!
We are adept at lighting fires,
This won't our minds ignite.

Doubt is always forefront
They don't like what is new,
Suspicious minds are thinking
This is the devil's brew.

They'd celebrate a baby,
Now here comes the catch,
They really have no interest
In the lighting of a match.

Da can see its uses,
Roger is quite proud,
Claire will use them always,
They voice support aloud.

A fiery re-creation,
Its history will cast
A trail of destruction
From the future to the past,

Fergus Man!! (s6 e2)

Fergus man, where are ye,
The bairn is on the way
Ye should be there beside her,
Not hiding away,

Fergus man, get up there,
Put the bottle down,
Yer wife could be in danger,
Stop acting like a clown.

Marsali does not need me,
She'll be fine with Claire,
She will not even notice,
If I am not there,

Fergus man, she calls for you,
She needs you by her side,
Get off your arse and be the man
Who took that girl to bride?

The birth does not go easy,
Her husband should be there,
You will nae forgive yerself
If she thinks ye did not care,

Fergus man, sober up
Ye whisky sodden tool,
Must I take ye there myself,
Ye wee Parisian fool.

She loves ye man, she calls for you,
Things are not tae plan,
Get yersel tegither
Ye aggravating man.

Roger laid the law down,
Took Fergus by the scruff,
Hot foot back to Marsali,
Will he be soon enough!!

The Right Hand of the Lord (s6 e3)

He'd sat and waited patient
Amongst the drama of that day,
His reasons kept close to his chest,
Would make young Malva pay.

No longer could he wield the strap,
He would not spoil the child!
Spare the girl the punishment,
For her mother being beguiled.

He would have the surgery,
And he would take the pain,
Repair his hand so he may have
The use of it again.

Jamie pinned him to the chair
And read aloud the Psalms
The right hand doeth valiantly
Tom Christie has no qualms.

The papist and the Protestant
Both quote the word of God,
Screamed aloud through gritted teeth,
Would often sound quite odd.

Soft words for the sutures,
We're round the final bend,
Walking in Deaths Valley,
The lords house at the end.

Silken stitches finished,
The end of my endeavour,
Just as they reached those pearly gates,
To dwell within forever.

Goodness, oh and mercy,
May help him through these pains,
They are but words, they do not live
In Thomas Christie's veins.

Pain Relief (s6 e3)

A stubborn man, set in his mind
Tis the healing craft of witches,
To feel no pain, the sleep of death,
To wake up then, with stitches.

He did not trust, he had no faith,
Though faith had set his mind,
He'd not submit to witchcraft,
In that way he was blind.

He sat there stoic in the chair,
Reciting Bible verse,
While Jamie's strength held muscle still
I heard Tom Christie curse.

No Leather strop between his teeth,
He screamed for all his worth
Through gritted teeth he called his Lord,
Questioning his birth

The operation simple,
But off the scale of pain
To free the tendons of his hand,
So, he could write again

And so, I operated,
Between two stubborn men
Neither one was giving in,
A respect was born right then.

Biblical his knowledge
Of Presbyterian curse
Tom Christie used the whole damn book
As the pain got worse

He could have taken ether,
But that would take some trust,
He'd rather sit and curse the Lord,
And suffer as he must.

He floats (s6 e3)

He Floats
He is the devil's spawn
Pipes a child's voice
A babe set in a basket,
He had little choice

He floats
The current takes him,
Drifting in the race,
Spinning in the eddies
Gathering in pace

Rising
From the water
A monster from the deep
Strong arms hold him safe and sound
His life will not be cheap,

Child
I baptise thee,
The father and the son,
His name is Henri-Christian,
And he is mine for one,

Protection
Would you harm a child?
Baptised for the Lord,
Harm him, the devil take ye all
Roger gives his word.

Touch him
He is flesh and blood,
Human just like you,
And remember that God watches,
All you little heathens do.

Wisdom of Solomon (s6 e3)

Himself
He laid his parlour out
Tables set with care,
The choices and the consequence
Not one would he spare.

Sinners
Lined before him
Faces white with fear,
The poker turning in the ash
Glowed white, their skin to sear

The Choice
The voice was calm, words dripped in ice,
Would turn their bowels loose,
Touch the bairn or touch the fire,
Tis up to you to choose,

Step Up
Watch, he is a boy like you
He gurgles and he grins,
Make him smile, look after him,
He is innocent of sins.

The Message
One by one they touched him
Saw him smile, and laugh,
A baby in a blanket
His size different by half.

Remember
He is a child of God
Do this all will be fine,
And remember Henri Christian
Is also kin of mine!

Consequences
They stood in line, hearts quaking
The consequences dire,
Lesson learned, they filed out
Not one had touched the fire.

And....

Germaine he is your brother,
He will need your protection,
Look after him, always
Shield him from rejection.

The Word

He said we would be damned to hell
Baptised him for the Lord ....
Mr McKenzie – is a man of God
Do not doubt his word.

Reward

Wisdom is a fine thing,
There's risk and there's reward,
And there is bread and honey
With the Bible and the sword.

Toil and Trouble (s6 e3)

I came upon him in the woods,
The man they call Himself,
I wandered, picking mushrooms,
Stealthy as an elf.

He does not know I watch him,
I see his every move,
My mind's eye maps his body
Covets every groove,

He is a man of honour,
He would do what's right,
He could be led into our trap,
Would he even fight.

My wiles could draw him from her,
Send her to the grave,
Be his comfort in his grief,
Then he'd be my slave.

Sister this is not the plan,
Tis I you take to bed,
The child is mine, you are mine,
no more to be said.

I loved you since you were a bairn,
We saw our mother die,
Who cared for you in those dark times,
Who heard your every cry?

Father tried to change you,
He tried to cleanse your soul,
Listen well and serve the Lord
Always hide our goal.

I would get us free of him,
Live our lives alone,
Without the pious ranting
His loud religious drone.

Sister you must not be swayed,
Commit the lies to mind,
Smallest detail proves your case,
See what you can find.

Father then and mistress,
Fevered like to die,
I'd comfort Mr Fraser,
Pursue the darkest lie.

My sinfulness is then revealed,
In words so meek and mild,
I'll only tell this to 'himself'
I'm carrying his child!

I'd watched him in the river,
Bathing with the men,
That tiny scar upon his arse
That was the one ye ken.

That fine lean muscled body,
Bears scars he wears with pride,
But that wee one, cannot be seen.
Tis hidden from the eye.

A bite scar soon forgotten,
A small knot in his skin,
Will prove to some I tell the truth,
But have I lain with him?

Coming Home (s6 e4)

They took me in, they made me theirs,
To them I gave my soul
There I loved a woman,
She that made me whole.

Their God, he who sees everything
Saw it was not right,
My spirit did not meet with hers,
Mine would not win the fight.

My child, one I called Ishabael,
Was buried with no name,
I never even saw her,
Dead before she came.

They cast me out, sent me back,
Go live with my kin,
Family is where ye come,
For they must let you in.

Uncle, where do souls go
Is she condemned to roam?
Must she wander endlessly
Nameless with no home,

We knelt beside the river,
We talked of what God planned
That Faith was there beside her,
Would find her, take her hand.

Her spirit was not nameless
Her name was in his heart
He would hold her sacred,
Her journey home would start.

A name is not what matters,
I have used more than a few,
Who you are is in your heart,
Your deeds are what marks you.

To do what's right when all is lost
When all you feel is pain,
Forgive, allow the sores to heal,
'T Will go against the grain

Find the way to ease your mind,
Accept God has a plan,
Lord knows we may not see it yet,
You will be the bigger man.

Calls in the Forest – a Cry for Help
(Book version)

Sat around the fire,
The pipe had gone around,
Stories told of battles,
Some fought on far off ground.

Beer and food and mellow smoke,
And talk of homeland lost,
I began to talk about that time,
The killing and the cost.

Fourteen men, I counted,
I could not call one to mind,
What sort of memory is this?
That makes such killing blind.

Back upon that rain-soaked moor,
My face with tears is sodden,
The earthy smell of peat and gorse,
Weeping for Culloden.

When all but Bird had gone to bed,
I told him of my fears.
That my women saw the future
The awful trail of tears.

Now Bird has sent his mother,
To warm me in my bed,
This is no sense of humour,
She has come to clear my head.

Talk to me Bear Killer,
I will comb your hair,
I hear your words in any tongue,
Your mind I will repair,

The words came out in Gaelic,
To her I bared my soul,
The spectres Grief and Loss and Fear,
The things that kept me whole,

I felt my spirit rising,
And floating up above,
My voice came from a distance,
Softer than a dove.

They will no longer haunt you,
No evil in my heart,
Not here, not now, in this place peace,
At least that is a start.

She combed the tangles from my mind,
Healing words she spoke,
All thoughts of vengeance on that time,
Dispersing with the smoke.

A restless night
(Book Version)

Heads I win, tails you lose,
I always get the bed,
Ian's coin is loaded,
He sleeps on the floor instead.

Snowbird is a canny chief,
He asks the King for guns,
But his men will kill without them,
When more raiders come.

I was thinking of the feel of home,
And drifting off to sleep,
A strong light hand upon my balls,
Caused my mind to leap,

Hell, there's a woman in my bed,
Ifrin there may be two,
Nephew – tell them they should go!
I've no words for what to do.

I'm flattered that they honour me,
But I am not the King,
I would nae say I'm well endowed,
Hmmm tis nae small thing!

It's raining hard, they can'nae leave,
Uncle, they must stay,
And they are staying in yer bed,
I think ye'd better pray.

That night I hardly slept a wink,
I'd one hand on my kit
A man's cock has no conscience
Mine was fighting back a bit!

Lying flat upon my back,
I prayed for some restraint,
An Indian lass on either side,
And a cock stiff in complaint!

Goodbye Iseabail (s6 e4)

I watched the rivers endless flow,
The anger left my bones
Running onward to the sea,
Clear water over stones

I sat, I prayed, I talked with them,
The spirits of my life,
The Murray's and the Mohawk,
My daughter and my wife.

Some not dead but in my mind,
Constant in my brain,
Those that sought to comfort,
Those that caused me pain,

There I found forgiveness
There I found my soul
There I found an inner strength,
That thing that keeps us whole.

Emily no longer mine.
Be happy in your life
I wish you many children,
May all be free of strife.

And you my Mohawk brother,
Make sure you love her well
There is a small place left in me,
That would see you in hell.

Carved with love, I blessed the wolf,
I laid it in the race,
Baptised it for you Ishabael,
I never saw your face.

I leave you here with all our Gods,
Whichever one you choose,
I'm sure they are all really one,
Just seen from different views,

You are not lost and wandering,
Like some discarded wraith,
A guiding hand will find your soul,
My uncle sends you Faith.

The Call of Faith (s6 e4)

Iseabail, I see you,
A path for you is planned
In the world ethereal
Come and take my hand

We walk beside our kinfolk
We watch them from above,
Hold the prayers they send us
Answer them with love,

Fly with me in spirit,
We never shall grow old,
One day the quick will join us,
In Gods eternal fold.

Family awaits you,
Tiny Mohawk wraith
You will never be alone
Cousin, I am Faith.

Time on earth is transient,
Must always have an end,
Spirit has no boundaries
On Faith you may depend.

Trail of Tears (s6 e4)

What then will become of us,
When the wars are done,
When the Kings men have all gone,
And independence won,

Will they let us live in peace?
Not take away our land,
Must we arm ourselves again,
Make another stand.

The white man he wants everything
He takes without consent
He rapes the land of all its wealth,
His greed is never spent.

He takes our sacred mountains,
He kills without restraint,
No respect for bird or beast
Or for a man of paint.

My brothers they will send you far,
Make you leave your home,
Do not believe their promises,
They will not let you roam,

Independence at a cost,
What the sacrifice
For white men are not tolerant
Your lives will be the price.

Banished from your homelands
Away from all you know,
To barren land, not fertile plain,
And you will have to go

The journey will see many die.
Upon a trail of tears,
It will come, it has been seen,
I can't allay your fears.

Twenty Rifles (s6 e4)

Loaded on the wagon
Gifted from the Crown
Paid for with my hard-earned coin,
I could na let him down.

Bird will have his rifles,
Tested, cleaned and bright
Twenty will nae win this war
Nor even win one fight.

My part of the bargain kept
The Crown would add a twist,
The King requires loyalty,
An oath is on the list.

I can no longer hold my line
Walk between the fires,
I fear I must tell him now,
That most white men are liars.

Bird, my women have the gift
They see what time will bring,
A time of death and sorrow
But not brought by the King.

In sixty years, it comes to pass,
The trail on which they cried,
Sent to land so far away,
In thousands they will die.

Tell it in your stories,
Keep all this in mind,
When the time approaches,
Please be hard to find,

wise old Bird will sing this song
Its words will keep them free
Sons and then his grandsons
Will hide the Cherokee,

This wife of yours, you value her.
Bird asked the question bold.
She cost me nearly everything,
Her price is more than gold.

Now the time to make the move
To step across the wire,
March with freedom, March with hope.
Step into the fire!

Continental Congress (s6 e5)

We'll drink an ale, we spar with words,
A lining up of views,
Alliances are tested
Each man makes his dues.

Trust must be established
If treason is the game,
I ken they have nae met me
To Hartnett just a name.

To toast the King, with eyebrows raised
A look of great disdain,
His comrade can'nae hide his take
Allegiance can'nae feign.

Bona Fides established,
My colours at their mast,
The Continental Congress,
Has signed me up at last.

A world of secret meeting,
When treason is in play,
One man, I cannot meet his eye,
What must I tell John Grey?

My eye drawn to the fire,
Have I come too far?
Will I end like Bonnet?
Bollocks in a Jar.

Talking Bollocks (s6 e5)

Wrinkled, insignificant
Once his pride and joy
Nestled in his breeches,
Each side of his 'Le Roi'

Hairy orbs, once sae attached
His measure of a man
Protected and respected
And scratched because he can!

There above the fire
Labelled and displayed
Removed from reach of fishes
When his final act had played

A potted curiosity
Or a message to us all
Where some are plotting treason,
And others potting balls.

Tis said that brave men have them,
They boast about the size
I have nae yet heard Claire complain
Of what's before her eyes.

Floating now in vinegar
Not hung between his legs
Stephen Bonnets bollocks
Like a pair of pickled eggs

We talk independence,
Freedom from the Crown,
Does this await my testicles?
When they cut me down!

A White Rose for the British (s6 e5)

The whole of town is abuzz with life,
A welcome for a Scot
A migrant from the highlands
They will forget her not!

The men in full regalia
Tartan de rigeur
Ladies in their finest
A Ceilidh to be sure!

Those that can't remember
Love to reminisce
Those that charged the British guns.
Would give those tales a miss.

How to address a legend,
Just say hello is best,
She's really just a person
Just like all the rest

A legend of the '45
A white rose to the core,
Speaking now for loyalty
A turnabout for sure.

The Oath that we were made to swear,
An exodus unplanned.
Rebuilt lives and fortunes,
A new and restless land.

They will not fight for freedom,
They will fight to keep their lives,
The lands they farm, the wealth they've
earned,
their kinfolk and their wives.

They have no taste for rebellion,
For they have lost before,
They thrive on tales of glory,
Remember the last war.

The English took my freedom,
I'll not again wear chains,
If I must fight again for right
I'll face the guns again.

For I know Fionnaghal!
She talks a rare, good fight,
The Bonnie Prince would pay in gold,
Would she assist his flight?

But I have better anecdotes,
I've ones tae raise a smile,
Like the day she stole my bridie,
And I pulled her hair foreby!

We met when da was buying sheep,
On the Isle of Skye,
She was nae fair or gracious,
When she poked me in the eye,

A braw wee lassie with the grippe,
And a very runny nose,
And both of us just barely seven,
My first love I suppose.

Well Jamie are you blushing,
A childhood crush you said,
On wee Flora Macdonald
My! Your ears are turning red!

Light relief (s6 e5)

Pleasant waves of light relief
Inhaled with many sighs,
Breathe it in and it will ease
The pain behind your eyes,

It also lightens all your mood
It may just calm your nerves
Let you give your audience
Just what it deserves,

Ladies come and join me,
Adjourn to pastures green
Where we can talk, and smoke the hemp
And do so quite unseen.

Giggling with laughter
The pipe was passed around,
Together with the hip flask,
The gossip did abound,

Talk of lives forgotten
The hemp removes a blind
Memories of darker times,
Hiding in your mind.

I am the sweet sleep calling you
Come then take a drop,
Reach out for my bottle,
I hear the stopper pop!

A small trip to oblivion
Will send the demons back,
A few drops on your handkerchief,
Will get you back on track.

Back before they miss you,
But miss you someone will,
Small lies you tell he will add up
Then will he love you still?

The Pen and the Tar Brush (s6 e5)

The bucket and the sweeping brush,
The pistol and the sword,
The latter are more fitting
For an English Lord.

He swung the broom most artfully
Painted men with tar,
More used to portraits done in oils
They would leave no scar.

Defender of the common man,
Upholder of the law
Honour bound to action,
His fighting arm is sure.

When all around is chaos,
When lawlessness abounds,
The seed to pillage others wealth,
Takes root in fertile ground.

A stronger force than honour
Holds these two together,
The traitor and the English Man
Bound as friends forever.

Back-to-back and side by side,
They will defend what's right,
A mattress full of feathers
Will help to end the fight.

A willow broom on outstretched arm,
Hot tar at its point,
Reenforced with Highland wit,
The raiders they'll anoint.

And when the fight is over,
The skirmish is all done
The victory is toasted,
Tis just lads having fun.

Aye Lord John I've missed ye too,
Ye've been busy I can tell,
If I just insert yon brush,
Ye may sweep the floor as well!

Tar and feather bed
(Book version)

Unrest settled on the air,
It hung upon the mist,
Pervasive as the fever
Persuasive as a fist

Change was starting to appear,
Collecting heavy dues
Driving good folk from their homes,
Punished for their views,

The smell of tar was cloying,
The mob was out for blood,
Fuelled by tavern gossip,
They gathered in the mud,

The printer was in hiding,
The shop they sought to burn,
Jamie stood there, broom in hand,
And fought each one in turn.

He swung it in a fiery arc,
Warrior's eyes were gleaming,
Tar was sticking in his hair,
Sweat down his face was streaming,

Joking with the hecklers,
Grandstanding the mob,
Daubing everyone with tar
He saw it as his job.

The crowd was growing restless,
They'd take him with a rush,
Then my Scottish hero
would get tarred with his own brush.

The Devils Pact (s6 e4)

Enquiring mind,
Intelligent
Quick to learn her work
Enthralled
Enthusiastic
True colours soon unfurled,
Curious,
And watchful
Sharp of hand and eye,
Nothing good
Will come of you
If through the latch you spy.
Watching
stolen moments
Noting every act
Plotting
Scheming
In your mind
With the devil makes your pact.

The Venom of the North Wind. (s6 e5)

Dabbling in witchcraft,
Meddling with charms,
Seeks to pull another's man
Into her vengeful arms,

A grave disturbed, Some stolen bones,
Seaweed burned in fire,
Take the ash and sprinkle
To hold your heart's desire,

An ancient love charm seldom used,
But where is it directed,
Who calls on these unholy words,
And who will be affected.

An old man's grave, but newly sealed
Remains fresh in the ground
Earth disturbed to find his bones,
To turn a head around.

The venom of the north wind,
Will blow cold across the land
Will raise a storm and break the peace,
If all goes as she's planned.

They say that what is bred in blood,
Comes out in the bone,
Scheming child born of a witch
Cannot her sin atone.

She will tear a home apart,
Will weave a web of lies,
Frasers Ridge will fall in flames
When Malva Christie dies.

There can be no justice
Where there is no law,
And lives are tossed like flotsam,
On the rising tide of war.

Desecration (s6 e5)

A poor old man, and wasted
His flesh hangs from his bones,
Now dead inside his shelter
Safe from praying crones,

Fed with sins ate from the dead,
A withered corpse his plate,
Life extinct will no one care,
Is he missing from Gods slate?

Was it sin that killed him?
Or maybe something worse,
A fever strong that has no cure
An apprentice witches curse.

Bread and ale they fed him
To keep Gods wrath at bay
To let the dead, lie peaceful
Their sins he'd take away

Sinister Miss Christie,
You've learned a lot I fear,
Your teacher gives you knowledge,
Your mother the idea!

Evil comes in many forms,
The devil drives your deeds,
What is it that you really seek?
What will fulfil your needs.

Morals of an alley cat,
Behaviour of a whore,
Spreading rumour on the ridge,
Damaging for sure.

Nought good will become of it,
When the good have been misled,
To save a life inside you
She will desecrate you dead.

The web you spread around you,
Will weave an evil tale,
Your mentor thrown into the fire
With stale bread and ale.

The Wind of War (s6 e5)

Feckless individual,
Driven low to crime,
Desperate for an Avenue
To get back to his time.

Imprisoned now, a common thief,
He will await his fate,
Stolen emerald in his hand,
His ticket home – too late.

Sitting in the shadows
The darkness of the jail
Killing time and waiting
His mission doomed to fail

Help me fellow traveller,
Would she help him from this spot?
How can he send a message?
Advertise his lot.

A whisper of a marching song
Carried in the air
A memory from the future,
Faint and hardly there

The feet of other soldiers,
March to a different war,
The tune composed by Sousa
Not written yet, she's sure.

Shivers running through her bones
Sounds her ears can't find
Haunting notes that drift away,
Play tricks inside her mind,

Pointless death and wasted lives
History agrees,
And Colonel Bogey marches on
Whistled on the breeze!

The Blazing Shits (s6 e6)

They never miss a Sunday,
Not seen for a week
Five wee bairns and counting,
They lie there, cheek to cheek.

Crows circle the cabin,
Flies buzz round the door,
The heavy cloying scent of death
Creeps across the floor

Dysentery, the blazing shits
For this there is no cure,
Save wash, and boil the water
The rest you must endure.

Sickness in the water,
Find the cause, we must
The graveyard fuller every day,
The reaper is not just.

Whole families lie dying,
Wracked with griping pain
The body tries to purge itself
Wants to be whole again.

Thirst and dehydration
They drink what made them ill
Death's circle is a vicious one
Bad water, it will kill.

I am fed up with funerals,
Of grieving for the lost,
We keep on boiling water,
And count the human cost.

Fever
(Book Version)

A child as young a Jemmy,
A father wracked with grief
I fell amongst the mourners,
Like an autumn leaf,

Exhausted, weak, failing,
Fever boiled across my brain,
With sparks of white-hot lightening,
Harbingers of pain.

My skin was tight and brittle,
flesh had burned away,
Pounding blood rang in my ears,
My body baked like clay,

Throat is tight, I cannot breathe,
I cannot take in air,
Faces, voices come and go,
But do not stop and stare,

I reached up and I touched it,
The beam above my head,
My fevered mind reminds me,
It's eight feet above the bed.

I hear voices calling
I must obey them all
Golden eyes the same as mine,
Implore me heed the call.

Braced against the window,
His face lit by the dawn,
Tears of grief run down his face,
A man prepared to mourn,

I only know I love him,
But I don't recall his name,
The amber voice still draws me in,
Will she win the game?

A figure stands beside him,
Her actions draw my eye,
That touch spurs my decision,
I'm not prepared to die

A Cool Haircut (s6 e6)

Don't look in the mirror Claire,
You'll surely have a shock,
They've scalped you like an Indian would
They have nae left a lock!

Would ye like a hat now Sassenach,
Tae cover up the mess,
That would stop me laughing,
Ye look funny I confess!

Shorn just like a highland sheep,
At least yer heid is cool,
Now put that knife down Sassenach
Din'nae play the fool!

A Kerch makes ye respectable,
A hat would hide the crop
I'd love tae see ye wearing
Some lace perched on the top.

I would na care if you were bald,
Your beauty is inside,
You're still the Claire I lay with
When ye were a bride.

Pardon me for laughing,
But ye really are a sight,
Shall I get yer scissors
And try tae put it right.

Would ye like a whisky
Before ye have a look,
short hair could be a fashion,
No – do not throw that book.

Kindly stop yer laughing,
You irritating Scot,
Hair will grow when it's cut off
I bet your balls will not

Jamie – go and do some work,
Tormentor of my soul,
And take your hats and kerches
And cram them up yer hole.

Faecal matter (s6 e6)

With jar in hand, I braved the walk
Tom Christie had the same,
Headaches and dry fever
Our guts did not inflame.

A prudish over pious man
Of women he was shy,
He thinks I do not know my place,
Thinks I come to pry.

Shorn of crowning glory
Hat upon my head
He looked at me as one he thought
Had risen from the dead

Enquiring of his welfare,
I went into his lair,
And ask him for a sample,
I baited god's own bear.

How dare I be so personal
It's as if he doesn't shit,
Would he put some in my jar?
He'd have none of it!

Madam I will take you home,
I will not have this talk,
You are weakened from the fever,
You can hardly walk.

I know you mean no harm in it,
This very strange request,
You will examine nought from me
I think ye need more rest.

Woman you are unseemly,
Your hair shorn like a monk,
What you ask is much too much
I fear you might be drunk.

I crammed my hat upon my head,
It's angle I arranged,
Tom Christie proudly walked me home
Some men will never change

Dirty Washing
(Book version)

An interrupted breakfast,
The Christie's came en-mass!
Well – there was the three of them.
Father, brother, and the lass

All in consternation
Tom was in a snit
He finds his daughter is with child
He'd find the truth of it

I took them to my study
Sat them down tae talk,
The Lass will only speak tae me
Or from it she will balk

A sense of dark foreboding,
Settles on the room,
Lies start flowing from her lips
Accusation's loom

She weaves a likely story
A good liar uses fact
But twists it to her own device
To bolster up her act.

Clever in her construct
She hangs her story out,
Careful that it fits the line,
Her dirty washing out!

That feeling in yer stomach
When ye step into a void,
When all your world turns upside down
She warmed and she enjoyed

Accused of taking her to bed
When my wife was sick
Seeking comfort from her
It cut me to the quick

Not just the once but several times
She said I'd sought her out,
The shock now turned to anger,
But the Christies did not doubt.

She described my body,
She itemised my scars,
Not just the ones upon my back,
The small one on my arse.

Even I'd forgotten
that spider bite was there,
A small round scar upon my rump
Condemned me then and there.

Would I put my wife aside?
And take this girl instead
Or they demand I keep her
If I will nae wed

Demand the child inherit
I must take it in,
I could kill Allan Christie
He is right under my skin.

Claire slapped her – made her ears ring
And then ran from the room
I know that I must find my wife,
She's out there in the gloom

And Mrs Bug brings whisky
The good stuff to be sure
To ease my anger and my shock
She heard all, outside the door

Claire is staring at the pool
Sat underneath a tree,
Does she doubt my faithfulness?
Does she believe in me!

She'd seen the shock upon my face
She knew it for the truth,
I'd never thought to bed that lass,
And rob her of her youth.

No good will surely come of this,
Gossip feeds on scandal
Folk will believe the Christie's
This one will be hard to handle

In time the truth will all appear
Til then we ride the wave
That little witch has sown a seed
And we Frasers must be brave

Ringing in the Ears (s6 e6)

Do my ears deceive me?
Lies are all I hear,
Corroborated clever lies,
Trouble brews, I fear.

How dare she speak of him like this,
My right fist starts to cramp,
She's spread her legs for someone else
Morals of a tramp,

Lying scheming alley cat,
Her brother eggs her on,
Her father must believe her,
And he must believe his son.

'Sir how could ye treat me so'
'He could not get enough'
So, help me shall I slap her now,
Or wait for his rebuff.

The arm that wields the pestle
Unleashed from my control,
All my strength behind it,
Landed on its goal.

A little out of practice,
Long since I threw a dish,
I haven't slapped a living soul
Since Jamie and that fish!

I set her ears ringing,
My throwing arm unfurled
Released a sound that Outlanders
Would hear around the world.

Scales of pain (s6 e6)

Delirium and fever,
A snake inside my brain,
Scales of red not healing blue
And never-ending pain.

I saw all things in shadow,
Yet crystal clear as day,
Dry the heat that seared me
Foreboding here to stay

A serpent lives inside my home
Reptilian, sly and sleek,
It spreads a poison through our lives
Not time to turn a cheek.

I saw you at the window
Bottle in your hand,
Helplessly I saw her there,
I saw her make her stand.

Do I know you, Jamie Fraser?
Must I spell it out,
Remind you I'm not from this time,
I cannot cope with doubt,

Cards upon the table now,
For I must be quite sure,
If she comes near my family,
I shall kill the stinking whore

We will ride a wave of hate,
Vicious rumours spread,
Truth will out, it always will
But someone will be dead.

Faithfulness (s6 e6)

Yer fierce as a badger,
More grizzly than a bear,
Prouder yes than lucifer,
And now ye have no hair,

Patience – ken ye have none
Kindness – din'nae jest,
Yer terrifying ruthless
When yer at yer best.

Female attributions
I fear that ye have none,
Well, none that I can count on,
Now yer arse is skin and bone.

I can'nae list yer virtues
All I need tae know,
Is you are there beside me,
And that ye'll never go.

Yer verra kind and verra clean,
But not much of a cook,
I've seen ye burn the supper
Yer nose stuck in a book

Should ye die and leave me,
I should be very sore,
I'd argue with the devil,
Tae let ye live some more.

Hair will grow, flesh will return
Your beauty will not fade,
You still outshine the sun itself
Ye put it in the shade.

Eyes like well-aged whisky
With a dash of honey
Ye tend to my wee scratches
Sometimes ye think me funny!

What is it draws me to ye?
Well, all of the above,
Yer faithfulness above them all,
And loyalty, and love.

A Moments Rest (s6 e6)

Voices hide in cupboards
Ghosts invade the air,
I hear them, and I look for them
I see they are not there.

My helper calls,
my faithful mask
A moments peace
Is all I ask

I cannot face this music,
Too much in my mind,
Sweet sleep and oblivion
My refuge I must find.

A few sweet drops
Upon the mask
I will find my peace
At last

Am I old and withered,
That she would have my life,
This house, my home, my everything
She wants to be his wife.

Devoid of life
Her body lies
Her throat laid open
to the skies.

There is no happy ending
Someone wanted blood
And Malva Christie's body
Lies lifeless in the mud,

Murdered
Life taken
All will be
Mistaken

The child lives, I feel it move
I can save its life
Surgery in the garden
With a pruning knife

Elbow deep
Blood and shock
Malva on
The butchers block

Not a pretty picture
They will not understand
Demented woman murders child
The blood is on my hands.

A Warped Mind (s6 e6)

Who knows the depths a mind can plumb?
When it comes to schemes,
This child I'd taken to my trust,
Had schemed beyond my dreams.

A web of lies so complex
It sounded like the truth,
Complete in minor detail,
Which in her mind was proof!

A bid to take my husband.
To ruin people's lives,
I could feel the gossips,
Sharpening their knives.

Her father – rightly angry,
Her brother – fit to kill,
Jamie – livid to his core,
Malva - lying – still.

I found her in my garden,
Throat slashed with a knife
Her babies heart still beating,
I tried hard to save its life.

Only time will find the truth,
Our lives are put on hold,
To serve a warped and twisted mind,
And someone's thirst for gold.

Rough Justice
(Book version)

I found her in the garden,
Throat slit, already dead,
Still warm, her blood still flowing,
A deathly shade of red.

My knife already in my hand,
I'd thought to find a bear,
Stealing all our honey,
Not Malva laid out there!

I saw her child still moving,
I could never do it harm
It's first and last breath taken,
In the shelter of my arms.

My knife cut swiftly through her flesh,
To open up that tomb,
A scrap of warm humanity,
Rescued from her womb.

It would have been so different,
Had the child survived,
The actions of a healer,
Thanking God, I had arrived.

Instead, I'm loading weapons,
There's a mob outside our door,
But I've survived one witch trial
I can survive one more.

Richard Brown wants vengeance,
Christie mourns the bitch
Jamie called the murderer
I am once again the witch.

I should have left her lying
Not even stopped to pray.
Hippocrates was far too strong
For me to walk away.

Lost Soul Remembered (s6 e6)

You learned, I taught,
You schemed and thought,
You planned and you betrayed,
I trusted you,
I cared for you,
All that was false you played.

I still can't see you evil,
Though all around me do,
Even at your violent end,
I tried to rescue you.

You learned my ways,
You learned his too,
You looked into our life,
Was it really in your plan,
Evict me – as his wife.

Oh, child of rare intelligence,
For no one is born bad,
I found out from your father
The start in life you had.

119

Endless curiosity, Was all of it a sham,
You think he would have kept you,
My honourable man,
Another child that is not his, Was it all part of
your scam.

You truly thought of everything,
Except that grain of good,
The one seed that was in your soul,
To treat me as you should,

You tried to put it all to right
Refused to follow through,
You died for that,
I know that now,
Your brother murdered you.

Your soul lies in my garden,
Buried in the weeds,
Your body in the graveyard,
Where it cannot plant more seeds.

I still come here and think of you,
Your child I could not save,
My lessons about saving lives,
Near sent us to our graves.

You never saw the hatred,
When they came to take us down,
Lives destroyed one fiery night,
At the hands of Richard Brown,

You sent us on a journey,
Which should end in a noose,
Released a tide of anger,
Which never should break loose.

But we are back We are as one
And stronger than before,
Battered at the edges,
Forged harder by a war.

Our bond is one you could not break,
It is not of this life.
Time itself has not the power
To split him from his wife

Shamed (s6 e7)

Congregation hear her!
She does not tell you lies,
False tears running down her cheeks,
Her innocence defies.

Seduced by one she trusted,
One who should have cared
One who promised kindness
Looked for how she fared.

She does not name her lover,
Not before this crowd
The lie is told to him alone,
His name she speaks aloud.

Her words are truth, as spoken
If you know the man
But will mislead, and will cause pain
It's all part of the plan.

Her baby is a bastard,
It will not bear a name,
The man who is the father,
Cannot announce his claim.

A brother who looked after her,
He who should be kind
Who nursed her as a baby,
A sinner we shall find.

In anger he protests too much,
He makes too much demand
His jealousy of Frasers life
Will overplay his hand.

She would not maintain the lie,
Her life pays for the truth,
Mind tormented, filled with guilt,
She'll sacrifice her youth.

Her father has suspicions
The lies he cannot stop,
But deep inside he knows the truth,
We hear the penny drop.

Trouble in Spades (s6 e7)

We would see her buried,
Would see her soul with God
They would lay her body
In un-consecrated sod.

I would wash her sins away
I would sew the wound
I would wrap her in her shroud
To lay her in the ground.

They would spread the rumour
They would twist the truth,
Say I wash my guilt away
Along with Malvas youth.

We will hold a service,
Roger will say prayers
They will say I am to blame
Corrupting one of theirs.

Circumstance against me,
The evidence is scant,
But all believe us guilty
I've nothing to recant.

Hiram Crombie spread his seeds,
Word poison sown with care,
He will not speak them to your face,
He would never dare.

Action and reaction,
If Allan is so shocked
Why take the coffin to your breast,
Your arms around it locked,

Malva was your sister,
Reaction says she's more,
Why are you weeping for her child?
Yet call its mother whore!

The truth will shame the devil
Time will bring the proof
Meanwhile trouble comes in spades,
And heaps upon our roof.

Gall berry Ointment (s6 e7)

Mistress ye were all away,
The Malaria came on,
My teeth were clacking fit tae break,
I needed something done.

The twins they know my ointment,
And they know what to do,
Rub it in all over,
Mistress I tell ye true.

Gall berry is such smelly stuff,
They could'na stain their sarks,
So, they took their clothing off
Preventing stains and marks.

I was cold, they kept me warm,
"Twas comfort in their touch
Mistress I was fevered
Did I enjoy myself too much?

I woke and saw his chest, all hair
Soft and curled like down,
Mistress it was lovely
Please mistress do not frown

His paps like tight wee raisins,
Right before my eye,
I never felt so safe before,
Oh, mistress please don't sigh

I can'nae tell the difference
Two bodies and one soul
And yes, it was the both of them
They are what makes me whole

Oh, Lizzie you must make a choice,
Or you may face a scandal,
Mister Fraser will take action
If tis more than he can handle.

Keeping a lid on things (s6 ep7)

I have na felt like this in years
My heid boils fit tae burst,
Christie's first, now Beardsleys
Which ones are the worst?

Keep yer temper Fraser,
Will not do to lash out,
Though you may wish to throw yer fists,
And feel the need tae shout,

Ye set yerself as man in charge,
Here your word is law,
Take a breath, and count tae ten,
Then search your inner store.

Anger calm and surgical
Like Claire would use her knife,
Find a cure with cutting words,
It may preserve a life.

All may yet be straightened,
With Lizzie and the lads
Ye, see she loves both Beardsleys
Can both of them be dads.

Ye said yer piece, ye made yer point
And then they found their priest,
The best they could short notice
"Twas Roger Mac at least.

I can'nae kill the both of them
And lay them at her feet,
They've pulled a fast one on the Laird,
Their solution is quite neat.

I think I can'nae worry,
it is nae worth the time
Far worse things will happen,
Is theirs such a crime?

If we stay whole throughout this mess,
For I can hear deaths drum
I need my anger all intact
To fight what is to come!

What's a bit of bigamy?
In the realm of all these sins,
And I can'nae tell the difference
Between the Beardsley Twins!

Unholy Trinity (s6 e7)

A furtive knock in darkness,
Three figures in the night,
Seeking out a minister,
To save them from their plight

They have a plan, it just might work
Though himself has spoken,
Catch the preacher unawares
Only just awoken!

Please marry us, pleads Lizzie
I find myself with child,
I do not want a scandal,
The mistress will go wild.

Kezzie is our witness
Please marry me and Jo.
I'm sure of what I'm doing
I really love him so!

It will nae be a marriage,
But I'll handfast ye tonight,
It's a binding union
Tis valid in Gods sight.

But let me put my breeks on,
I've no time tae prepare,
I can't conduct a wedding
While my arse is bare.

A trinity unholy,
Most masterful of schemes
Both twins are in the eyes of God
Hand fast to Lizzie Wemyss!

Over Your Shoulder (s6 ep7)

I see you Mrs Fraser
Trying to do good,
Knives so sharp and words to match
You do more than you should.

I watch you mistress healer
I haunt your every day
I live inside your conscience
I will not go away.

Hedgewhore, you had it coming
You got what you deserved
Corrupting our good women,
We had our justice served.

Hear me Dr Rawlings
The consequences fear,
Our wives are property to use,
You should not interfere.

You see me in your surgery,
You feel me in your house,
As you creep for your 'cup of tea'
Quiet as a mouse.

I am the voice inside your head,
That calls you to that mask
The sleep that makes you rid of me,
The Oblivion you ask.

A shadow in your surgery,
Your sanctuary breached,
Nowhere now for you to hide
Where your soul cannot be reached.

So run to that great man of yours
The one that is your world,
I follow close upon your heels
While in his arms you're curled

There will be a vengeance,
It will ride into town,
My brother, he will keep his word,
Beware of Richard Brown

Little Boxes. (s6 ep7)

Folded up and packed away,
The troubles of the past
Every small mistake I made
From first one to the last.

Sealed inside an inner wall
The box lid nailed down tight
Stored away in corners dark
Far away from light.

With hollow voice he reaches
Breaking through the dark
Lionel Brown is whispering
His taunting leaves its mark

No longer hiding from me
His calling becomes bolder
All the past he waves at me,
His ghost is at my shoulder.

Every life I ever touched,
Every life I changed
He turns the good to evil,
All is rearranged.

All I did for love of you
Is trampled into dust,
No longer can I face myself
In the mirror of the just.

Never ending voices call
And I do what they ask
Just one drop and then one more
Take refuge in the mask.

I see your eyes awash with tears
As I push you away,
I'm fighting what I have become,
My demons out to play.

Easier if I were gone
It is as if I lied,
I thought the thoughts, but not the deed
The day that Malva died.

A cup of tea will cure all ills
The kettle calls the pot,
Blackness fills my very soul,
I'm English not a Scot.

Sassenach don't fight me,
There is refuge in my arms,
Not bottled in your surgery,
Break free of ethers charms,

All the good that you have done,
Is here before your eyes,
How can ye think so foolish lass,
Ye are intelligent and wise,

The ridge exists because of you,
And may God damn their soul
It's you who heals their bodies,
Keeps their families whole.

Let me fight your ghosts my love
As you fought mine before
I will confront the devil
Should he turn up at our door

Hear the echo of the past,
He will do what he must,
The time has come and Richard Brown
Will turn the dreams to dust!

Superstition (s6 e7)

Gripped in superstition
Fear of the unknown,
The seed of hate is planted
And soon enough it's grown

Deep in soil of ignorance,
Watered then with doubt,
It pokes its shoots up to the sky,
A weed you should pull out.

Choking truth, like bindweed
Propagating fear
It sees just what it wants to see
Hears what it wants to hear

Healing becomes witchcraft
Good deeds become a crime,
Stubborn and reliant
On tales from olden time.

Every slight is magnified,
Every fault is grown,
Fingers point and tongues will wag,
The gossip weed is sown.

Where is knowledge when you need her,
To know the hearts of men,
And the wicked tongues of women,
Whose talk is cheap – ye ken

They will sit around their kettles
Throw snippets in with pride,
What they knew of Malva
The facts will be denied

They covet all that has been built
Envy fuels the flame
Religion the accelerant,
To destroy the Fraser name

For every truth there is a lie,
For every lie a reason.
No evidence to prove a crime,
The Fraser hunting season

Bolt the Door – again (s6 e7)

He heard it first, the rumble
The hooves across the ground,
The clink of harness and of guns
A distant chilling sound.

I saw his eyes flash steely blue,
Unreadable his mask,
Intruders come into our life,
My defence his task

Pulled up outside of rifles range,
That voice rang in my ears,
This committee is not safety,
It brings my greatest fears.

The gloating words, the challenge
Enjoyment in our strife,
Richard Brown announces,
That he's come for Frasers Wife.

My wife is not a murderer,
Ye will nae take her in,
It's not her crime tae answer for,
This is not her sin.

No evidence but gossip,
No proof but idle chat,
Ye are nothing but a lynch mob,
A vengeful one at that.

Load the guns now Sassenach,
Tis time tae go to war,
And for a different reason,
It's best we bolt the door!

Surety (s6 e8)

Innocence protested,
Death the Browns had planned
Tom Christie entered in the fray,
And offered out a hand,

Justice his if anyone's,
Malva was his child,
He would see us safely,
There would be a trial.

His hair unkempt, his beard long
He walked an old man's walk,
But took command and saved our lives,
Made sense and justice talk.

One last night in our own bed
Under our own roof
He'd escort us then to Hillsboro
And a trial to find the truth.

Jamie still would fight the world,
And all that that entails
This man of words who spoke with sense,
Took wind from all Browns sails.

Tom Christie was our surety
To him it would endure
There would be no lynching
Before our guilt was sure

The start of a long journey,
To try and prove our case,
Now living in a lawless land,
Where justice hides her face.

Taken (s6 e8)

Shutters closed! Bolted tight,
Bar behind the door,
Rifles primed and loaded
Kept beneath the floor

We could hold out for hours,
Maybe not for days,
Food and water rationed
We shall see how this one plays.

Richard Brown seeks justice
No, he seeks revenge
He blames me for his brother's death,
And that, he would avenge.

He stands there waving flags of truce
His tricorn in his hand.
I'd shoot that hat from off his head,
Before I leave my land.

I mark the line with rifle fire,
A line he will not breach,
Come no closer, lest ye die.
Step into rifles reach.

Hiram Crombie offers words,
The Fisher folk are come
But burn the witch is all they want,
By the pricking of my thumb.

Burn the witch, avenge the lass,
Bring out yer murdering wife.
Verdict reached without a trial,
Claire would lose her life.

And Allan Christie goads them
Seeks vengeance for his kin,
I think that he protests too much,
Not devoid of sin.

Loaded in a wagon,
Taken from our home,
Where are the folk we needed?
Now for Justice we must roam

Scales of Justice (s6 e8)

I cannot see this woman hanged,
Her skill before it's time,
Is healing wounds and curing ills
Really such a crime?

I do believe in witches,
She is not one of those,
She has a rare intelligence
A calling I suppose.

And he inspires loyalty
Men follow him to die,
A man of honour bound by truth
I've never known him lie.

And then I fear I know my son
A weak and snivelling liar,
A sneak thief and a coward
won't set the world afire.

Jealousy lives in his soul,
He has no sense of pride,
Envy curdles all his deeds
And gnaws at his inside.

And then I know the devils get
Her blood is of a witch,
Her mother was a sorceress
My wife the whoring bitch.

The Lord will see that truth is out,
The devil put to shame,
Papist, Presbyterian
Our God is one – the same.

And should the Lord be tardy,
In putting things to right,
I will see that justice
Fights the Frasers fight.

A man who takes a flogging
To spare one mad and old,
Whose wife returned in all those years,
Would never break his code.

An educated woman,
Duped by the witches' mind,
Has walked into the fire of hell
Her kind heart made her blind

The Ridge is made of simple folk
They fear the unknown
Superstition justifies
The evil seeds they've sown.

Brown would have a hanging
He has vengeance in his soul,
A personal vendetta
The gallows are his goal.

Tom Christie looked into his heart
With love where all else fails,
He added truth to justice
And balanced up the scales.

Only I can heal this wound
Be the bigger man,
I must step in Frasers shoes,
And fill them if I can.

Gone (s6 e8)

Jamie!
Overpowered,
He fought, there were too many,
Then a gun butt to his head,
The world went black around him
Then I thought him dead.

Jamie!
Do not take him
You said we'd go together,
Liars all, you bastards,
You won't defeat us – ever.

Tom
Where is my husband,
Is he still alive,
If he is dead, there is no hope,
I cannot survive.

Trust Me
Mistress Fraser,
He looked into my eyes,
Trust the Lord, trust what is right,
I will not let you die.

Find Him!
No! I stay with you,
To you I gave my hand,
He is alive, I know him well
Survive what they have planned,

Tom
What are you not telling me,
Tell me what they've done,
Tell me where they've taken him
Or I really can't go on.

Days on days the wagon drove
Looking for the law,
Broken towns and broken lives,
We saw the start of war.

Now bars and locks and darkness
Will they break me, I can't tell
My mind goes back to Wentworth,
A prison, yes, and hell

Head lice (s6 e8)

Wee crawlers, hiding in his hair
Young Jemmy he has lice,
Picked up from the fisher folk,
I didn't check them twice,

Sit ye down my little man,
Time tae cut yer hair,
Yes, I fear it will be short,
Just like granny Claire.

His lovely locks fell to the floor,
With lice they were alive,
Crawlers running for the door
Clean up on aisle five!

What is this mark upon his scalp?
A nevus small and red,
Just above his wee left ear,
A mole, here on his head.

It's nothing tae concern ye,
I'm sure I have one too,
Growing here under my hair,
I was five before it grew.

They say they are inherited,
A coin begins to fall
This shows that Jemmy is his son
Now no doubt at all.

Sit down man and brave the shave,
You two can look as one,
Shorn like sheep, and granny Claire
Roger and his son.

I fight with you (s6 e8)

There was but a second
Before the world went black
When silent death, swift as the wind
Started our fight back

Planning to deport me,
To Scotland – on that ship,
Losing Claire was losing life
Losing every grip.

Light on the air and silent
They rained their arrows down,
Christ Ian lad ye took ye time,
My breeks were turning Brown.

Bear killer, now I fight with you
Browns henchmen died in sand,
Cherokee with rifles,
Chief Bird makes a stand.

I will die another day,
The fight will still go on,
Can ye tell me someone, please
Where my wife has gone.

Din'nae shoot the last one!
Oakes – he will know where,
The bastards that have taken her
Have hid yer Aunty Claire.

I hope they've hid her safely
Or she will run for the hills
She's very likely wandered off,
To doctor someone's ills.

Uncle we ken where she is,
We din'nae need this scum,
A rifle shot straight through his eye
Blows Oakes to kingdom come.

Horses gallop down the beach,
Their destination where?
We wait for season seven.........
Will they rescue Claire?

Jamie and Claire's Theme
Alternative words to the Skye Boat Song

Time will flow on,
When we are all gone
Our love will never die,
Two hundred years
It will always be strong
Two souls as one my dear

Blood of my blood
Bone of my bone,
Travelling down the years,
Holding you close
Feeling you strong
Smoothing away your fears.

Time will not dim
Years will not age
Your beauty will never die
Sassenach Lass here in my arms,
Forever and e'er to lie

Ghostly I came,
Calling your name
Hoping you'd be my soul,
Spirit in chains,
Purgatory claims
True love will keep us whole

Blood of my blood
Bone of my bone,
Travelling down the years,
Holding you close
Feeling you strong
Smoothing away your fears.

We will go on
Til all life has gone
A love that does not enslave
Powerful love as lasting as ours
Truly transcends the grave

Acknowledgements

As always, I acknowledge the amazing work of Diana Gabaldon without which this homage would not be possible.

The work of the writers' producers, actors and production crew of Starz and the Outlander Team.

I will also mention my home-grown editing team who exist on social media and pull me up on my punctuation and grammar, content and accuracy and occasionally make very pertinent suggestions. I take all your criticism in good heart and will usually act upon it. I do not stretch to an editing team; I am a one-man band on a shoestring.

Special mention here for Caleb Reynolds to whom I dedicate the poem, Fisher Folk. He is the young actor who plays Aiden McCallum in the series. I'm sure he has a bright future ahead of him.

And to Hanca Forch for allowing me the use of her photo edit as a cover image.

Copyright

Other books by the author

This book is the eighth book in a series of Unofficial Books of Outlander inspired poetry.

Unofficial Droughtlander Relief.

The Droughtlanders Progress.

Totally Obsessed.

Fireside Stories.

Je Suis Prest.

Après Le Deluge

Dragonflies of Summer

Semper in Aeternum

The Blue Vase - In Hardback and Illustrated

I hope the Princess will Approve – a book of COVID and Horse related poems.

· ·

Ginger like Biscuits - the adventures of a Welsh Mountain Pony.

Rhymes and Rosettes

Pixie Saves Christmas

RDA

It's what you can
do that counts

Riding for the Disabled Association
Incorporating Carriage Driving

Made in the USA
Columbia, SC
08 May 2022

60015857R00100